THE
WRITING WARTHOG

MODERN CURSIVE WRITING FOR GRADES 4-6

WRITTEN & ILLUSTRATED BY BEV ARMSTRONG

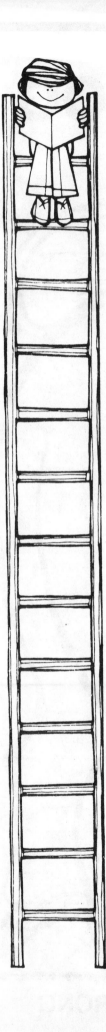

The Learning Works

Using the Writing Warthog

1. The alphabet chart on page 3 shows the correct formation of all letters in the modern cursive style. Each page also features a properly drawn letter, with an arrow showing where to begin when writing it.

2. Each page has a space which a student may practice writing a letter in upper and lower case, first by tracing dotted lines and then freehand.

3. Each page also features a sentence for the student to copy.

4. On page 56 are hints on how to avoid common problems in cursive writing, plus a checklist which students may use when evaluating their work.

Copyright © 1995-The Learning Works, Inc.
Santa Barbara, California 93160
Printed in the United States of America
ISBN 0-88160-243-4

Cursive Alphabet

abcdefghijklmnopqrst!

Aa Bb Cc Dd Ee
Ff Gg Hh Ii Jj
Kk Ll Mm Nn
Oo Pp Qq Rr
Ss Tt Uu Vv
Ww Xx Yy Zz
0 1 2 3 4 5 6 7 8 9

A a

a a a a   a a

a a a a   a a

Amanda, an acrobatic anaconda, balanced on Ana anteater's back.

Á a

a a a a

a a a a

Aaron Aardvark ate an awesome amount of animal crackers.

$\mathcal{B} \mathcal{B} \mathcal{B} \mathcal{B} \mathcal{B}$

$b \; b \; b \; b \; b$

Beneath a big baobab,
busy baboons bought
bagels for breakfast.

NAME

B B B B

b b b b

In his bathtub, Boswell
blew bubbles at some
nearby bumblebees.

C c c c c

c c c c c

Clarice Chinchilla can color while chewing on a candy cane.

C c

C C C C

c c c c

A cockroach escaped from the cuckoo clock in Chuck's clubhouse.

$\mathcal{D}d$

$\mathcal{D}$ $\mathcal{D}\mathcal{D}\mathcal{D}\mathcal{D}$

d $d d d d$

Twin dik-diks dashed across the desert to Djibouti at midnight.

NAME

D D D D

d d d d

Mudskippers danced
in the middle of the
puddle at daybreak.

E-l

E E E E l

l l l l l

Each of the huge emu's
eighteen eggs broke
when she sneezed.

NAME

$\mathcal{E}\,\mathcal{E}\,\mathcal{E}\,\mathcal{E}$

$e\,e\,e\,e$

Three eager egrets went speeding east to Erie, seeking free ice cream.

$\mathscr{F}\,f$

$\mathscr{F}\,\mathscr{F}\,\mathscr{F}\,\mathscr{F}\,\mathscr{F}$

$f\,f\,f\,f\,f$

Five fireflies flew in formation around a frustrated flamingo.

F f

F F F F

f f f f

The puffin stuffed
herself with fresh fish,
then failed to fly.

$\mathcal{G}\mathcal{g}$

$\mathcal{G}\,\mathcal{G}\,\mathcal{G}\,\mathcal{G}\,\mathcal{G}$

$g\,g\,g\,g\,g$

Hang gliding over the
gorilla, George Gecko
swigged ginger ale.

G g

G

g

Giggling galagos in the jungle grab grasshoppers to gobble.

H h

H H H H

h h h h

Hannah Hammerhead
chomped a huge chunk
out of Hank's ship.

H h

H H H H H H

h h h h h

In Hilo, Hawaii, three
hyenas in hula skirts
dashed to the beach.

Ll i

l l l l l

i i i i

In Illiopolis, Illinois,
little lizards like to
lick dripping icicles.

$\mathcal{I} \, i$

$\mathcal{I} \, i \, i \, i \, i$

$i \, i \, i \, i$

Zip, the indri, swings
wildly on ivy vines
with his sister, Izzy.

J j

J J J J

j j j j j

By a Jamaican jail, kinkajous joined jays for a game of jacks.

$\mathcal{J}\ j$

$\int \int \int \int \int$

$j\ j\ j\ j\ j$

Jogging past a juke box, a jaguar jauntily juggled jelly beans.

K k

K K K K

k k k k

A sneaky kookaburra kidnapped Kudzu, king of the katydids.

NAME

$KKKK$

k k k k

The kangaroo's frisky
king snake snuck
out of her pocket.

$\mathscr{L}\,\mathscr{L}$

$\mathscr{L}\,\mathscr{L}\,\mathscr{L}\,\mathscr{L}$

$\ell\,\ell\,\ell\,\ell$

Lively lemurs loped
along the jungle trail,
alarming armadillos.

$\mathcal{L}\ \ell$

$\mathcal{L}\ \mathcal{L}\ \mathcal{L}\ \mathcal{L}$

$\ell\ \ell\ \ell\ \ell$

Lolling on a limb of
the laurel tree, a lazy
lion lapped lemonade.

Mm

M M M M

m m m m

MMMMMMMMMMMM MM MMMMM MMMMMMMMM

Mog, the mad mantis,
hummed merrily while
chomping on moths.

M m

m m m m

m m m m

How many mittens
must I make for my
millipede, Mortimer?

NAME

nnnn

nnnn

Norwegian newts snack
on frozen bananas and
crunchy onion rings

N n

n n n

n n n n

The numbat sang his country songs each night in Nashville.

Oo

Ooo

oooo

Only ocelots wore good waterproof boots in the cold October floods.

$\mathcal{O}o$

$\mathcal{O}\,\mathcal{O}\,\mathcal{O}\,\mathcal{O}$

$o\,o\,o\,o$

An obnoxious ostrich in Congo swallowed forty-four coconuts.

P p

p p p p

p p p p

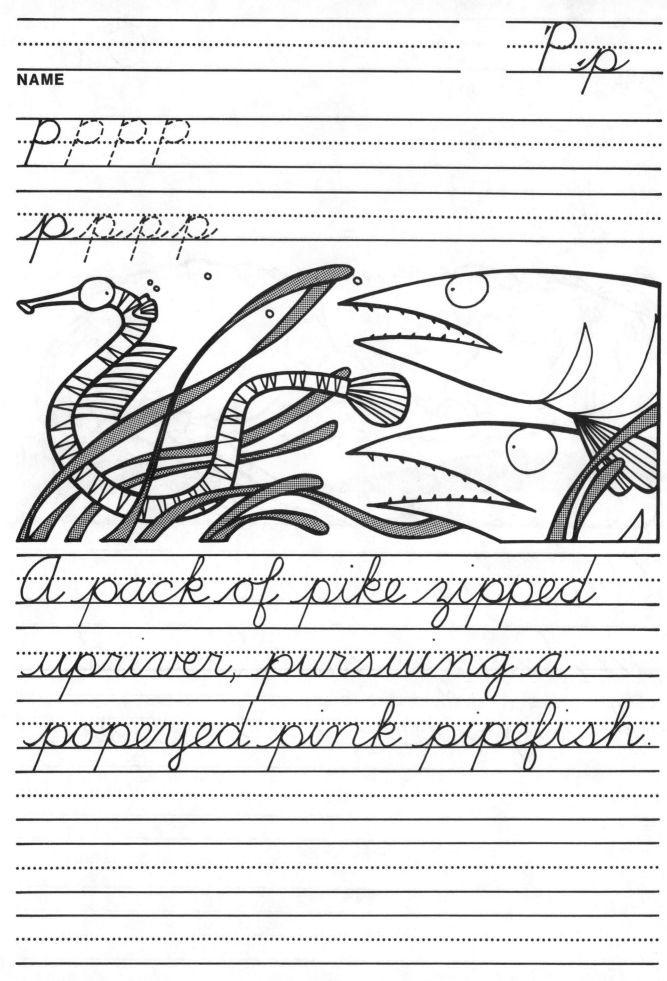

A pack of pike zipped

upriver, pursuing a

popeyed pink pipefish.

P p

p p p p

p p p p p

Pat Platypus pitched a
pineapple pie past the
hopping opossums.

2*q

2 2 2 2

q q q q

Quivering quietly, the
squid squeezed a quart
of loquat juice.

2.q

2 2 2 2 2

q q q q q

Quick quetzals catch mosquitoes near the squishy quagmire.

R r

R R R R

r r r r

Radical roadrunners
in Reno run around
rather recklessly.

NAME

R R R R

r r r r

The rocket-powered red
reindeer roared forward,
releasing rare parrots.

S s

S s s s

s s s s

Sidewinders seldom spend their summers skiing in Sudan.

_S s_

_S S S S_

_s s s s_

Shaggy sloths, snoring noisily, sleep in Swiss sassafras trees.

$\mathcal{T}t$

$\mathcal{T}\mathcal{T}\mathcal{T}\mathcal{T}$

$t\,t\,t\,t$

The tiger bit a bitter trout, then spit it into his tiny tin tuba.

$\mathcal{T}t$

$\mathcal{T}\mathcal{T}\mathcal{T}\mathcal{T}$

$t\,t\,t\,t$

Tabasco, the tough toad,

was totally stuffed

with termite tamales.

U u

U U U U

u u u u

Unruly young kudus slurp plum pudding in buckets, burping loudly.

$\mathcal{U}u$

$\mathcal{U}\,\mathcal{U}\,\mathcal{U}\,\mathcal{U}\,\mathcal{U}$

$u\,u\,u\,u\,u\,u$

Toucans in Uruguay

guzzle gallon jugs of

cucumber juice.

$\mathcal{V}\kern-2pt v$

$\mathcal{V}\,\mathcal{V}\,\mathcal{V}\,\mathcal{V}$

$v\,v\,v\,v\,v$

Vera Vulture hovered over the Volga River, viewing olive groves.

V v

V V V V

v v v v v

Various vipers living in Vesuvius, Virginia, are vegetarians.

NAME

W W W W

w w w w w

Two weasels warily watched a wet walrus swallowing pawpaws.

W w

W w w w

w w w w w

Wes Warthog waltzed westward, waving two willow switches.

X x

XXXXX

X X X X

Max, an excited fox in
Xilitla, Mexico, fixed
his extra taxi.

Xx

XXXXX

XXXXX

Did the ibex expect
that extra box of wax
crayons to explode?

Yy

Y Y Y Y

y y y y y

Yellow-eyed coyotes yodel nightly among the yuccas in Yuma.

Y y

Y Y Y Y

y y y y y

The crazy yapok was trying to fly a toy yacht yesterday.

Z Z

Z Z Z Z Z

Z Z Z Z Z

The zany zebus from Zanzibar play jazzy Zulu cadenzas.

ℨℨℨℨℨ

ℨℨℨℨℨ

Zombie, the buzzard, lazily blew his kazoo while eating pizza.

Writing Warthog Checklist

1. Are your letters the correct <u>height</u>?

fox   *fox*

2. Is each letter <u>shaped</u> and <u>slanted</u> correctly?

pike   *pike*

3. Is there <u>space</u> between the letters and words?

a jay   *a jay*

4. Are all letters resting <u>on the base line</u>?

emu   *emu*

5. Is your writing <u>neat and clean</u>?

toad   *toad*

Warthog Hang-ups

Watch for these problems as you write.

a   o a
<u>a</u> written like <u>o</u> or <u>u</u>

i   e
<u>i</u> written like <u>e</u>

d   cl
<u>d</u> written like <u>cl</u>

b   li
<u>b</u> written like <u>li</u>

r   r r
<u>r</u> written like <u>i</u>

h   h have
<u>h</u> written like <u>li</u>